# In Like
# a Lion
# Out Like
# a Lamb

# In Like a Lion
# Out Like a Lamb

by **Marion Dane Bauer**

illustrated by **Emily Arnold McCully**

Holiday House / New York

March comes with a roar.

He rattles your windows

and scratches at your door.

He turns snow to mud,
then tromps across your floor.

March comes with winter clinging to his tail.

He scatters sleet

and sometimes even hail.

"Were you expecting spring?" he snickers.

"Reach for your slickers."

March comes with a pounce and a growl.

Just step outside and hear him howl.

If you howl back,
will he go away?
Not very likely!
This lion means to stay
and stay
and stay.

Then one soft morning
wind gives way to breeze.
Buds pop out on trees.
The air is full of chickadees
and bumblebees.

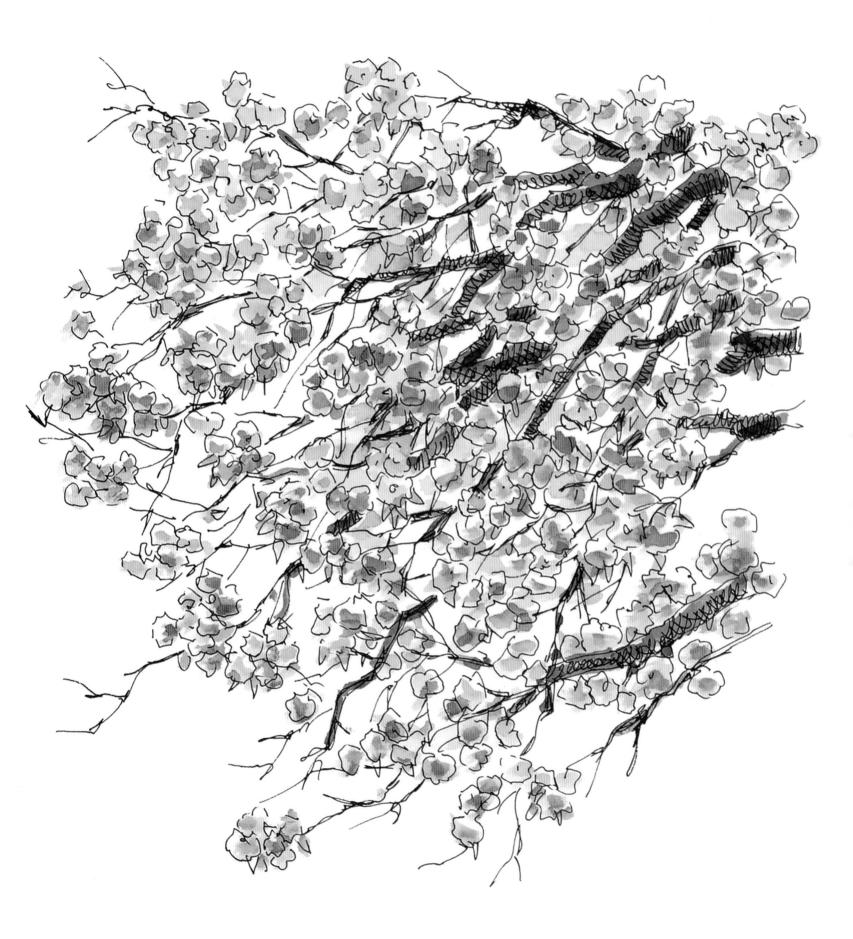

And the lion takes a whiff, a sniff,
and lets out an enormous sneeze.

And guess who
comes riding in,
gliding in,
striding in
on that A-A-A-A-CHOO!

So . . .

where will the March lion go?
Will he wander to and fro,
defeated and lost,
predicting frost?

Or will he skulk through the greening grass,
eyes scheming,
teeth gleaming,
waiting for the lamb to pass?

No, never!

This fellow is much too clever.

He finds himself a sunny spot.

He stretches, yawns,

and curls into a knot.

And that rumbling noise you hear?
Never fear.
This lion is done with roaring,
and now he's snoring!
At least until next year.

Today the lamb's in charge
of grass and flowers,
sunshine and showers;
of babies,
small and large.

Come, all you babies.
Just hear March sing.
"Ba-a-a-a!" she says.
"Ba-a-a-a!" and "Ba-a-a-a!" again.